THE CAT-ASTROPHE

Written by **Katherine Kearney Maynard**   Illustrated by **Bailey Watro**

AuthorHouse™ LLC
1663 Liberty Drive
Bloomington, IN 47403
www.authorhouse.com
Phone: 1-800-839-8640

Illustrated by Bailey Watro

Published by AuthorHouse 09/05/2013

ISBN: 978-1-4918-0934-1 (sc)
ISBN: 978-1-4918-0933-4 (e)

Library of Congress Control Number: 2013914992

authorHOUSE®

For Heather,
a girl who loves cats

In summertime, this last fine year,
The cats all got together.
From feline mouth to feline ear
The word was always "Heather!"

For cats, my dear, have understood
And get the word around
When someone's kind and sweet and good,
With her will cats be found.

So, from the South, from East and North,
And even from the West,
To Heather's house they scampered forth;
They'd heard she was the best.

3

Now, Heather lay upon her bed;
She dreamed of handsome boys.
But then the visions in her head
Were shattered by a noise!

It sounded like some kind of purr,
But louder than was fitting.
It sounded like a cat to her,
A cat the size of Britain!

So, puzzled and a little scared,
She crept across the floor;
She gathered up her nerve and dared
To open up the door.

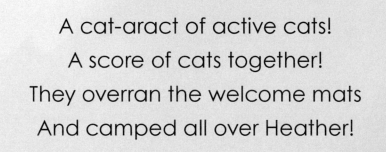

A cat-aract of active cats!
A score of cats together!
They overran the welcome mats
And camped all over Heather!

Proud Manxes, cuddly Russian blues,
Sweet tabbies brown and red,
Soft tortoiseshells of varied hues
All walked on Heather's head!

The Turkishes, Egyptian Maus,
Sleek Korats (with soft fur)
All piled into Heather's house
And romped all over her.

A giggling Heather then arose
From this great pile of fur.
Cat hair was on her clothes, her nose,
In fact all over her.

Then, careful not to step on tails,
She went to take a bath.
A walking fur-ball, she left trails
Of cats' hair in her path.

9

She shed her clothes and ran the bath,
Then settled down to scrub.
But, oh! With purrs, meows, and gasps,
The cats raced to the tub.

They formed a little cat-tub-ring;
A furry, purring crowd!
When Heather started in to sing,
The cats joined in! And loud!

They made a cat-aclysmic sound
Like all the world's babes bawling!
Their yelpings echoed round and round;
They made a cat-erwauling.

When she got out, they used their paws
To dry her off and warm her.
They brushed her hair with careful claws,
Then sat in catty-corners.

Then Heather dressed and told her friends,
"I know what we can do.
Let's play until the daylight ends!
I've wished for cats like you!"

Then play! They jumped like acrobats;
They rolled on the pool table.
When they got tired of this or that,
They slept in a cat's-cradle.

They played with yarn, they played with string,
They played with nuts and bolts.
They played with any little thing;
They played with cat-apults.

They chased around the kitchen floor;
They cat-walked on the gutter.
They opened up the fridge's door;
They licked up all the butter.

They turned cat-wheels, and Heather clapped,
They found the house's fun spots.
If they grew tired, they just cat-napped
(Preferably in sun-spots).

They crawled through basement cat-acombs,
Exploring every nook.
(Unchecked, a kitten always roams
Where nobody would look.)

When Mum came home, what did she see?
A hundred cats together!
She cried: "What's this? Cat-astrophe!
I'd better talk to Heather."

When Heather told her Mum the facts
Of the great feline invasion,
She said she'd care for all the cats;
She spoke with great persuasion.

So Heather, to this very day,
Inflates the swimming pool,
And fills it up, up all the way,
With cream that's sweet and cool.

For meals, they sit in one great line
In front of many dishes.
On fish and beef and cheese they dine;
Their meals are quite nutritious.

When Heather sleeps, the kittens make
A blanket of their fur.
And every morning, when she wakes,
Her cat-friends welcome her.